THE GREATEST

ALAN GIBBONS

With illustrations by
Dylan Gibson

To Anthony Walker

First published in 2006 in Great Britain by
Barrington Stoke Ltd
18 Walker Street, Edinburgh, EH3 7LP

www.barringtonstoke.co.uk

This edition first published 2014

A CIP catalogue record for this book is available
from the British Library upon request

ISBN: 978-1-78112-364-5

Printed in China by Leo

Contents

Chapter 1
Enemy No.1

My name is Ali

My hero's name is Ali. He is Muhammad Ali. He's the greatest boxer who ever lived. His poster's on my bedroom wall.

I'm 12 years old. I live in England.

Muhammad Ali was born on January 17, 1942 in Louisville, Kentucky.

That's in the USA.

I'm a Muslim. So is Muhammad Ali.

Some people blame Muslims for all kinds of things. It was the same for Muhammad Ali. I've had to learn to fight, just like him.

I'm fighting tonight against St John's Club. They're the best club around here. I'm fighting their best boxer. That makes him the best boxer in this area. There will be three rounds. I feel sick. Yes, I'm sick with nerves.

Muhammad Ali started boxing when he was 12. Somebody stole his new bike so he went looking for a policeman. The cop was called Joe Martin. When Muhammad Ali found him, Martin was teaching boys to box. Muhammad Ali liked what he saw and joined in. One day he would be the greatest World Heavyweight Champion ever.

Someone stole my bike too and I know who did it. It was a boy called Chris Keane. He stole it when I was riding it. He was with his gang. They pushed me off my bike and took it. The next week, I started boxing so no one would ever take anything from me again. Tonight I fight Keane. One of us will be the area champion. I hope it's me.

Keane hates Muslim kids. He hates anyone he thinks is different. He picks on kids with red hair or glasses. Most of all, he picks on kids like me. He calls me a Paki. He says I'm a terrorist. He says I'm like Osama bin Laden. But I'm no terrorist. I'm 12! I'm just a normal kid. I like football, computer games and boxing. I just want to be left alone. I want to be a man of peace. I want to be like Muhammad Ali.

I start packing my stuff. See, my hands are shaking. I look up at my poster of Muhammad Ali. 'Did your hands shake, champ? How did you feel before a fight?' I wish you could tell me.

"Are you ready, Ali?" Dad calls.

"Yes, I'm coming," I tell him.

I look at the poster of Muhammad Ali again. 'Wish me luck, champ.'

I jog down the stairs and follow Dad to the car. It's a taxi. That's what Dad does for a living. He drives taxis round town. He's been called a Paki too. He doesn't fight. He says it's best to ignore the men who say it. He doesn't like trouble. Neither do I. But I'm not going to walk away. I'm not going to let people take what's mine.

Dad starts the car. I watch the town flash by. That's the street where Keane took my bike off me. I got it back in the end. Dad sorted it out for me. He went round Keane's house and spoke to his dad. But the frame was bent. Keane did that on purpose. He wanted to upset me.

He did that all right. I felt ashamed. Dad shouldn't have to stand up for me. I should be able to do that for myself. I swore I would learn to stick up for myself. Tonight I will.

"Are you nervous?" Dad asks.

"Me? No," I say.

He knows I'm not telling the truth. My voice goes funny when I'm going to fight. It's OK once I'm in the ring. It's the bit before the fight, the build up, that gets to me. My hands go clammy. The back of my neck gets hot. Even my legs shake a bit. I feel as if I'm falling to bits. But I don't.

When I'm in the ring I'm cool. I hit fast and dance away. I've won all my fights this year. I'm like my hero Muhammad Ali – a winner. I remember what he said:

"Float like a butterfly,
Sting like a bee."

When Keane comes out of his corner, I'm going to float. When he gets tired, I'm going to sting. He won't hurt me. I won't let him.

At last, we're at St John's Hall. This is Chris Keane's home ground. He took my bike from me that time. He thinks he's hard. He thinks he can do anything to me. He thinks he's going to win.

But he's in for a surprise.

Muhammad Ali – The Early Years

Muhammad Ali was born Cassius Marcellus Clay on January 17, 1942 in Louisville, Kentucky.

At that time black people in many parts of the USA were seen as second-class citizens. They had to use different seats on the bus and in restaurants. They did not have the same right to vote as white people.

In 1954, when Muhammad Ali was 12, his bike was stolen.

He went to the police.

Officer Joe Martin said he would teach him to box.

By the time Ali was 18 years old, he had won two National Golden Gloves crowns and two National Amateur Athletic Union titles.

In 1960, when he was 18, Ali won an Olympic Gold Medal.

Chapter 2
Nerves

When I walk into the changing rooms Jerry
Feeney comes over. He's our coach. He was
a boxer himself. You only have to look at his
nose. One day he asked me why I wanted to
box. I said I hated Keane. Jerry said hate is for
losers. You have to love yourself. He showed
me how to get fit. I did press-ups and tuck
jumps. I did pike jumps and star jumps. I did
lots of stuff like that. He taught me to move.
He taught me not to lose my temper. He taught
me discipline.

"How are you doing, Ali?" he says.

Jerry doesn't care if you're a Muslim. He just wants you to be a good kid. That's what he always tells me and the other boys.

"Just be a good kid. Stay out of trouble."

I want to tell him I'm fine. But he'll know I'm lying.

"I'm nervous," I tell him. "I've got butterflies."

"Good," Jerry says. "You can use that. It will give you an edge. If you get too cool or too cocky, you lose. Look what happened to Muhammad Ali against Ken Norton."

I've seen the DVD. Dad bought them all for me – every fight Ali ever had. Norton beat Ali when Ali was getting old. Ali didn't train hard enough. He got lazy but he got punished for it. In that fight, Norton broke his jaw.

"Yes," I say, "Norton beat Ali but Ali got his revenge."

Norton beat Ali in March 1973. A few months later, Ali was back. He beat Norton in October the same year. Keane took my bike last year. This year I'll beat him. I don't hate him any more, but I won't let him push me around.

"Anyway," Jerry says, "get changed, son."

Dad takes the hint. He's the boss until I get to the gym. Then Jerry takes over. He's my boxing dad.

I can hear people coming into the hall. There will be five or six fights. All the boys' dads will be there. Then there are the coaches and some others. That's a lot of people watching. Now I'm more nervous than ever. My shirt sticks to my back. It's the sweat.

That's when Keane walks in. He's got his hair all spiked up, full of gel. He's done it just for our fight. He looks at me and grins. It isn't a nice smile. Then he carries on round the corner. He thinks I'm scared of him. He thinks I'm beaten already. I'm going to prove him wrong.

Some of the other boys try to talk to me.
I don't want to know. I just want to shut my
eyes and see the ring. There will be Keane and
me facing one another. He'll come after me.
Hunter and hunted. Predator and prey. I'll
have to dance. I'll have to bob and weave. He's
strong so I have to stay away early on. I have
to take the sting out of his punches.

"Make him work," Jerry says. "You're not
going to fight. You're going to box."

I nod. He's told me that before.

There are three fights before mine. I watch
the boys go out to fight. I watch them come
back. They're excited if they win. They look
let down if they lose. One boy looks as if he's
crying. He sees me watching and turns red. I
won't cry. I won't lose, that's why.

Hey, that sounds like one of Ali's poems:

"*I won't cry.*
I won't lose –
That's why!"

I go to pee. For ages it won't come. That's another sign of nerves. A member of our club comes in and looks in the mirror. His cheek is swollen and red.

"Did you win?" I ask.

"No," he says. "I lost. He was too strong for me. Keep an eye on Chris Keane, Ali. He's the best they've got."

I know that already. His dad was a boxer. So were his brothers. It runs in the family. All his family will be in the hall, cheering him on. I've only got Dad. Mum doesn't come. It wouldn't be right.

I wait until I'm on my own. I look in the mirror. How will *my* face look after the fight?

"Ali?" Jerry calls. "Anybody seen Ali?"

"I'm here," I say.

"Come and get your gloves on," Jerry says. "You're up next."

I nod. He's holding my boxing gloves. When I hold out my hands they shake a bit. He pretends not to see.

"This boy you're going to fight is a bully," Jerry says. "He's a bit like Sonny Liston was in the old days."

Sonny Liston is the guy Muhammad Ali beat to become World Heavyweight Champion. They say Sonny Liston hung around with gangsters. Everyone was scared of him. Not Ali. He beat Liston twice. He knocked him out both times.

"Bullies get beaten," Jerry says. "You've just got to use your loaf."

My loaf. That's what Jerry calls my head. He means I've got to box clever. No problem.

Muhammad Ali's Road to the Championship

October 29, 1960: Ali beat Tunny Hunsacker.

December 27, 1960: Ali beat Herb Sile.

January 17, 1961: Ali beat Tony Esperti.

February 7, 1961: Ali beat Jim Robinson.

February 21, 1961: Ali beat Donnie Freeman.

April 19, 1961: Ali beat Lamar Clark.

June 26, 1961: Ali beat Duke Sabedong.

July 22, 1961: Ali beat Alonzo Johnson.

October 7, 1961: Ali beat Alex Miteff.

November 29, 1961: Ali beat Willi Besmanoff.

February 10, 1962: Ali beat Sonny Banks.

February 28, 1962: Ali beat Don Warner.

April 23, 1962: Ali beat George Logan.

May 19, 1962: Ali beat Billy Daniels.

July 29, 1962: Ali beat Alejandro Lavorante.

November 15, 1962: Ali beat Archie Moore.

January 24, 1963: Ali beat Charlie Powell.

March 13, 1963: Ali beat Doug Jones.

June 18, 1963: Ali beat Henry Cooper.

February 25, 1964: Ali beat Sonny Liston to become Heavyweight Champion of the World.

ALI vrs LISTON

WORLD'S HEAVYWEIGHT CHAMPIONSHIP BOUT!!!

SEE THE BIG PUNCHES

FEB 25TH

Chapter 3
Face Off

When Muhammad Ali fought Sonny Liston they thought he had no chance. Liston was mean and tough. He was unbeatable. Bets were seven to one against Ali. Ali didn't care. He called Liston a big, ugly bear. Ali wore a robe that said, "Bear Hunting". Keane is a big, ugly bear too. I'm going bear hunting.

"Are you ready?" Jerry asks.

"I'm ready."

I follow him to the ring. I see Keane's dad and his brothers. They're smiling. They shake their heads. They're saying I've got no chance. I'm going to show them. I duck through the ropes and climb into the ring. When I lift my head Keane is looking right at me. His eyes are hard. I see his lips move. I know what he's saying.

"Paki."

I'm going to stop him doing that. I don't hate him. So why does he have to hate me? Why does he have to call me names? I've never done him any harm. I just want to be left alone.

I go to the middle of the ring. The ref explains a few things. We touch gloves and go back to our corners. In three rounds one of us is going to be area champ. I want it to be me. I want that so much. I want Keane to know I'm as good as him, maybe even better.

When the bell goes Keane comes out first. He rushes across the ring and starts throwing punches. They're wild and most of the time they miss. Lots of kids give up the moment Keane comes at them. He scares them silly. I'm different. I'm using my loaf. I dance away, just like Ali. I see Jerry nodding. 'Don't fight, box.' Keane comes after me. I jab at him, a left then a right. The punches don't stop him. He keeps coming. I keep dancing. I move round the ring, keeping out of the corners. I don't want him to trap me where he can land a punch.

One time I catch a word.

"Coward," he mouths.

I meet his look.

It means stand and fight. I glance at Jerry. I know what he wants. Don't fight, box. That's what I'm going to do. I'm going to stay away from Keane. I'm going to move. I'm going to outbox him.

Trouble is, Keane doesn't know that. He just keeps coming at me, like a big, ugly bear. He follows me the way Joe Frazier followed Ali. Smokin' Joe Frazier was the first man to beat Ali. That time, Ali wasn't just fighting Frazier. He was fighting the American Government too.

Ali had defended his title ten times. No one could beat him. Then the Government wanted him to join the Army. Ali refused. He said he was a Muslim. He wanted peace. America was fighting a war against a small country called Vietnam. Ali refused to go. So they took his title away. For over three years he wasn't allowed to box. He lost the best years of his sporting life.

When he was allowed to box again, he fought Joe Frazier. Joe was tough and hard to hurt. He followed Ali around the ring and knocked him down once. Ali got up. He went on boxing. After 15 rounds Ali lost on points.

Some people call it the greatest fight of all time.

I watch Keane following me round. He'd like to knock me down. He'd like to see me flat on my back. It isn't going to happen.

The bell goes. As we pass each other, Keane whispers, "Stand and fight, Osama."

I don't say anything. But I hate the way he calls me that.

Ali Loses his Title

After that first fight with Liston, Ali became a Muslim. He changed his name from Cassius Clay to Muhammad Ali. A lot of the newspapers hated him for that.

On May 25, 1965 there was a rematch with Sonny Liston. Ali beat him by a knockout in round one.

November 22, 1965: Ali beat Floyd Patterson.

March 29, 1966: Ali beat George Chuvalo.

May 21, 1966: Ali beat Henry Cooper.

August 6, 1966: Ali beat Brian London.

September 10, 1966: Ali beat Karl Mildenberger.

November 12, 1966: Ali beat Cleveland Williams.

February 6, 1967: Ali beat Ernie Terrell.

<u>March 22, 1967</u>: Ali beat Zora Folley.

Then, from 1967 to 1970, Ali was banned from boxing. He had refused to join the US Army.

He said, "Why should they ask me to put on a uniform and go 10,000 miles from home and drop bombs and bullets on brown people in Vietnam while so-called Negro people in Louisville are treated like dogs?"

In 1970 the American courts changed their mind. Muhammad Ali was allowed to box again.

<u>October 26, 1970</u>: Ali beat Jerry Quarry.

<u>December 7, 1970</u>: Ali beat Oscar Bonavena.

<u>March 8, 1971</u>: Ali lost to Joe Frazier over 15 rounds. It was his first defeat as a professional.

Chapter 4
Fists of Fury

At the end of the first round I go back to the corner and sit on my stool.

"You're doing well," Jerry says.

"He wants me to stand and fight," I say. "He's started calling me names."

"I'll talk to the ref," Jerry says. "That's not allowed."

"No," I tell him. "Don't. I don't want any help. I can beat him my way."

Jerry nods. "It's up to you, son."

He leans over. "But don't lose your temper," he says. "That's what the boy wants. He's clumsy. If you stand and swap punches, he'll win. But if you dance, you win. He's stronger but you're faster."

Jerry squeezes my hand.

"There's something else," he says. "I've noticed something."

"What?" I ask.

"When Keane throws his right hand," Jerry says, "he drops the left."

"So?" I ask.

"Simple," Jerry explains. "If you throw a right-hand punch, he's got no defence. You'll get him."

I tell him I'll remember. But when I get to the middle of the ring Keane's doing it again. He mouths an insult. The ref doesn't see. I stop moving and swing at him. The punch doesn't hurt him. But when he hits me back, it hurts like mad. I've been stupid. I'm not boxing, I'm fighting. He hits me in the ribs and I feel my legs wobble.

Jerry's saying something to me. "Dance." Yes, dance like Ali. I move away. It isn't easy. My legs feel weak. But I get away from him.

My neck's hot. I feel stupid. I fell for it.
Keane made me fight.

But it isn't over. Ali lost to Joe Frazier. But
he came back. He beat Frazier twice after that.
I'm not finished yet. I'm going to turn this
round.

I dance and Keane follows me. He catches me once but the punch doesn't land properly. I swerve and get away.

That's when I hear Keane breathing. He's puffing and panting. It's the first time he's looked tired. Hey, I could win this fight. I skip round him, jabbing. He's slowing down. He can't come after me the way he did. After two rounds of swinging punches he's running out of steam.

Muhammad Ali Takes his Title Back

<u>July 26, 1971</u>: Ali beat Jimmy Ellis.

<u>November 17, 1971</u>: Ali beat Buster Mathis.

<u>December 26, 1971</u>: Ali beat Jurgen Blin.

<u>April 1, 1972</u>: Ali beat Mac Foster.

<u>May 1, 1972</u>: Ali beat George Chuvalo.

<u>June 27, 1972</u>: Ali beat Jerry Quarry.

<u>July 19, 1972</u>: Ali beat Al 'Blue' Lewis.

<u>September 20, 1972</u>: Ali beat Floyd Patterson.

<u>November 21, 1972</u>: Ali beat Bob Foster.

<u>February 14, 1973</u>: Ali beat Joe Bugner.

<u>March 31, 1973</u>: Ali lost to Ken Norton.

September 10, 1973: Ali beat Ken Norton.

October 20, 1973: Ali beat Rudi Lubbers.

January 28, 1974: Ali beat Joe Frazier.

These 14 fights meant Ali could have another go at winning the World Heavyweight Championship.

He had to fight a former US Marine, George Foreman.

Everyone thought Foreman was unbeatable. He had never lost. He had won with ten knockouts in the first round, 11 in the second round and 11 in the third and fourth.

He'd also knocked out Joe Frazier and Ken Norton, two men who had beaten Ali.

The fight between Ali and George Foreman was held in Zaire, in Africa. They called it the "Rumble in the Jungle".

Ali surprised everyone. He didn't dance this time. He lay on the ropes and took every punch Foreman threw. He called it the 'rope a dope'.

In the eighth round Ali came off the ropes and knocked Foreman out.

He was World Heavyweight Champion for the second time.

Chapter 5
Final Countdown

It's the third and last round. Keane doesn't look happy. Jerry says I'm just ahead on points. My punches don't hurt Keane much but they score points. He keeps missing and I keep scoring. He's tired too. It's all that swinging and missing.

The bell rings for the round to start and we come out of our corners. I see Keane's dad and his brothers. They're talking about the fight. This time, they're not smiling.

Keane has to catch me and land some punches. I try to dance away. Trouble is, I'm

tired too. Keane catches me with a right hand.
I flop against the ropes and he moves in. He
hits me again.

I suck in my breath. Then I see Jerry.

"Dance," he says. "Dance."

I try, but Keane puts his arm round mine and swings me back. That's when I remember what Jerry said. When Keane throws his right hand, he drops the left.

He has no defence. I see him throw the right. So I lean back.

Keane's wide open. I put everything into a right-hand punch to the ribcage.

Keane gasps and stops dead. He's not smiling now. That's all I need. I skip away and hit him with a right and a left. They don't hurt but I'm off the ropes. I scored too.

Keane tries to follow me. He's swinging with both hands. Every time he tries to get me, he misses. Jerry's smiling. Keane's dad is shaking his head. Then I see Dad. It's the first time I've noticed him. He nods to me. I'm winning.

I remember something about Ali. A boxer called Ernie Terrell called him his old name, Cassius Clay, not Muhammad Ali. Ali beat him. After every punch Ali kept saying, "What's my name?"

As I skip past Keane I whisper in his ear, "I'm not Osama. What's my name?"

Then I hit him twice. Left, right. The punches aren't hard but they score.

The bell rings. The ref lifts my arm. I've won.

Muhammad Ali's Career Ends

<u>March 24, 1975</u>: Ali beat Chuck Wepner.

<u>May 16, 1975</u>: Ali beat Ron Lyle.

<u>June 30, 1975</u>: Ali beat Joe Bugner.

<u>September 30, 1975</u>: Ali beat Joe Frazier in the "Thriller in Manila". Both men said the fight was so hard they felt like they were dying.

<u>February 20, 1976</u>: Ali beat Jean Coopman.

<u>April 30, 1976</u>: Ali beat Jimmy Young.

<u>May 24, 1976</u>: Ali beat Richard Dunn.

<u>September 28, 1976</u>: Ali beat Ken Norton.

<u>May 16, 1977</u>: Ali beat Alfredo Evangelista.

<u>September 29, 1977</u>: Ali beat Earnie Shavers.

February 15, 1978: Ali lost his title to Leon Spinks. This was a big shock because Spinks was unknown. By then, Ali was 36 years old. People thought he was too old to come back again and become champ.

September 15, 1978: Ali proved them wrong. He came back the way he had after the Frazier and Norton fights. He beat Leon Spinks and took back his title. He was the first man to win the World Heavyweight Championship three times.

After that, Ali retired but came back and boxed again after 18 months. He loved the roar of the crowd too much.

It was a mistake. Boxers are young men. By this time, Ali was too old. He'd had too many hard fights. He lost twice then retired again, for the last time.

October 2, 1980: Ali lost to Larry Holmes.

December 11, 1981: Ali lost to Trevor Berbick. It was his last fight.

Later in life, Ali suffered from Parkinson's disease. Many people think this is because of all the punches he took to the head. All these years later, in spite of his illness, he is still one of the most famous men in the world. He lit the torch at the 1996 Olympics and led the American bid for the 2012 Olympics. He travels the world and everywhere he goes people want to hear what he has to say.

He is much more than just a sportsman.

Chapter 6
Result

Jerry puts his arm round my shoulder.

"You did well, champ," he says.

I like the way he says it. "Champ."

Dad comes over too.

"Well done, son," he says. "You didn't lose your temper."

"I did once," I say.

Dad laughs. "I know, but you got over it," he says.

I leave the ring and get changed. All the other boys come over to shake my hand or slap my back. This must be why Ali kept boxing. I feel like a hero.

We are walking to the car when Chris Keane comes over with his dad. My stomach turns over. I don't want any trouble.

"My son's got something to say to you," Keane's dad says.

Keane doesn't look too happy. His dad nudges him.

"Well done," Keane says. "You were the better boxer."

He grits his teeth. He doesn't like saying it. There's something else. He really hates having to talk to me about it.

"I'm sorry I said those things," Keane says.

His dad takes over.

"My son had no right to insult you," he says. "This is boxing, not gang warfare. It's meant to be a sport. Now shake hands."

I take Keane's hand. He doesn't smile. I don't think he's changed all that much. He'd still be a bully if he could. But there's something in the way.

Me.

I'm the greatest.

Muhammad Ali – The Greatest of all Time

Muhammad Ali won 20 World Heavyweight Championship fights.

For the years when he was fighting there were seven different US presidents.

He fought in a time when there were other great fighters. Men like Sonny Liston, Joe Frazier and George Foreman are legends too.

He's the only man to win three World Heavyweight Championships.

He won his third title when he was 36 years and 8 months old.

He gave up his first title because he thought the war in Vietnam was wrong.

He became a symbol of the fight against racism.

He became a hero to everyone – black and white people, Muslims and non-Muslims.

He wasn't allowed to box for three and a half years, but he still came back to win the title twice more.

Today he is one of the most loved athletes of all time.

The Things Muhammad Ali Said

"I'm so great, I impress even myself."

"I'm young, I'm handsome, I'm fast. I can't possibly be beat."

"Float like a butterfly,
Sting like a bee,
His hands can't hit
What his eyes can't see."

When asked, during his three and a half year lay-off, if he missed boxing: *"No, boxing misses me."*

After his "Thriller in Manila" with Joe Frazier: *"It was like death. The closest thing to dying that I know of."*

About war: *"How can I kill somebody when I pray five times a day for peace?"*

About refusing to join the army: *"I just wanted to be free. And I made a stand all people, not just black people, should have thought about making."*

About racism: *"But there's still hatred, and hating someone because of his colour is wrong. It's wrong both ways – it don't matter what colour does the hating. All people, all colours, got to work to get along."*

Muhammad Ali to Martin Luther King, the Civil Rights leader: *"In your struggle for freedom, justice and equality, I am with you."*

About retiring: *"Father Time caught up with me. I'm finished – we all grow old."*

Our books are tested
for children and young people by
children and young people.

Thanks to everyone who consulted on
a manuscript for their time and effort in
helping us to make our books better
for our readers.

More from *Barrington Stoke* ...

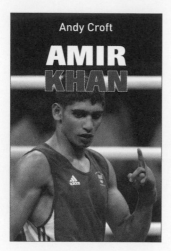

Amir Khan
ANDY CROFT

School boy boxer.

Silver medal at the Olympics.

World champion.

How did the boy from Bolton become such a superstar?

The Number 7 Shirt
ALAN GIBBONS

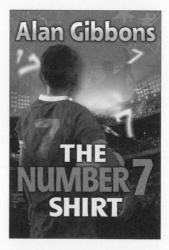

Football is Jimmy's life. When he gets into the Man U Academy, it's a dream come true – but he still has lots to learn. Lucky for him, he's got help ... his football heroes.

They all have one thing in common – the Number 7 Shirt. Will Jimmy win now he's got the help he needs?

Stat Man
ALAN DURANT

Arnie Keen is a real football boffin. He knows so many footie facts that his mates call him 'Stat Man'.

But then Arnie's team's star player is hurt, and Arnie has to take his place. Can Arnie cut it on the pitch?

And can the team still win the Cup?

Gold & Glory: Team GB 2012

The London 2012 Games were amazing for Team GB!

From Ellie Simmonds's speedy swimming to Mo Farah's amazing running ...

From Sir Chris Hoy's super cycling to Jessica Ennis's fantastic heptathalon score ...

Read all about the stars of the games and how they won their gold medals!

www.barringtonstoke.co.uk